MW00880103

Santa Baby

A Dickens Holiday Prequel - Dorrit's Diner

Peggy Jaeger

Published by Peggy Jaeger, 2021.

SANTA BABY

First edition. June 7, 2021.

Written by Peggy Jaeger.

To all the Foster Parents who open their homes and hearts to children in crisis and need. You are, truly, God's gift to humanity. Thank you.

Chapter 1

O n a cold Christmas Eve, 38 years ago, in the tiny New England town of Dickens...

Amy Dorrit considered it one of life's simple gifts that she didn't have to commute to work each morning. She could jump out of bed five minutes before she needed to be ready, and, courtesy of the shower she religiously took each night to rid her of the day's clinging aromas of grease and coffee, could simply run a quick washcloth over her eyes to rid them of the sleep nestled there. A dab of deodorant, a speedy dance with her toothbrush, and a tug of her waist-length, honey colored hair into a ponytail completed her morning ritual. She threw on her work uniform of old and much-loved jeans, t-shirt, and sneakers, before skipping down the thirteen steps from her apartment to the diner.

As the owner and operator of one of Dickens' favorite eateries, Amy turned the *closed* sign to *open* each day and then reversed the act every night. A dedicated work ethic had been instilled within her from watching her parents work tirelessly in the diner throughout her childhood.

She'd completed her homework sitting at the lunch counter every afternoon while her mom poured her a glass of milk and her dad cut her a slice of the day's pie. As a high school senior, she'd filled out her college applications sitting in one of the booths with her mother and her mother's best friends, Corrine and Matilda, looking on, giving sage advice and opinions. She'd bussed tables and learned how to brew a delicious cup of coffee before she learned to ride a bike. When she could be trusted not to burn herself, Amy learned to sling hash and grill a mouthwatering *Dickens Burger* the locals still asked for by name.

In the two winters since her parents' deaths within days of one another from the flu, running the diner and serving the citizens of Dickens consumed the bulk of Amy's life. To honor the parents who'd loved her unconditionally, and to keep their memories alive, Amy kept the diner flourishing.

On this cold Christmas Eve morning, Amy bounded down the stairs, her lips lifting at the knowledge Santa would visit the children of Dickens tonight. The smile broadened when she considered how long she could linger in bed the following morning since the diner would be closed.

And who she'd be lingering there with.

As she moved through the breezeway connecting the diner to her apartment, Amy heard a mewling sound at the back alley door. Her cook, Willie, often left scraps out for strays, especially in winter, and sometimes when she took the trash out at the end of the day, Amy would find a mamma cat searching for something to feed her kittens.

Amy opened the door, expecting to see a hungry animal looking for a handout, and got the shock of the century when she found a baby carrier, complete with a crying infant nestled in it.

She gasped, her head flicking right, then left, to find the person responsible for leaving a baby out in the frigid night air.

"Hello? Is anyone here?"

The still sleeping and silent town surrounded her as shoe impressions in the fresh snow indicated the baby hadn't been there for long.

The infant's howl echoed in the quiet.

"Oh, you poor thing. Let's get you out of the cold."

She brought the carrier into her small office off the diner's kitchen. Willie would be arriving within seconds so they could open at their usual time of 5 a.m. There were ten million things to get ready for the day before she turned the sign and unlocked the front door, but right now all her focus centered on the wailing infant.

After placing the carrier on her desk, she switched on the overhead light and spotted a piece of paper shoved into the blanket covering the child. Lifting the baby into her arms, she cradled it close. When she nuzzled her face against the little red cheeks, she gasped at how cold they were.

The hearty cries grew louder.

"It's okay, sweetie. It's okay. There's certainly nothing wrong with your lungs, is there?"

Once freed from the confines of the blanket, Amy realized the infant couldn't have been more than a few weeks old. Beet-red stains colored the tiny face from a mix of crying and the cold temps. Its fists flailed inside the white, full body bunting and a tiny knit cap covered the round head. Amy left it in place until the infant could warm up a bit.

"What in the name of all that's holy are you holding, Amy Dorrit?"

Willie Jackson stood at her office door, a lit cigarette dangling from a corner of his mouth, his leather jacket hanging open and his eyes as big and round as his county-famous blueberry pancakes.

"What does it look like?" Amy dug around in the carrier searching for a bottle, pacifier, *something*, to soothe the baby's cries. "Lose the cigarette. It's a baby and I'm pretty sure it's hungry."

He lifted those shocked eyes to Amy's face. "Girl, you been keeping secrets from ol' Willie?"

"Oh for Pete's sake. Are you nuts, William Jefferson Jackson? It's not *my* baby. I found it at the back door when I came downstairs."

"Whose is it?"

"No idea."

"*What* is it?"

Holding the small bundle like a football in one arm, she shoved the piece of paper she'd found at him. "Same answer. I haven't looked yet. Here, read this. I found it tucked inside the blanket." Once he had it, Amy placed her pinky finger over the baby's lips. It immediately rooted, then latched on to suck.

"I knew it. It's starving."

" 'I'm sorry,' he read aloud, 'but I can't take care of her—' well, we know it's a girl –'I have no job and no way to hold on to one with a baby. Please forgive me for leaving her like this, but I saw how kind you were yesterday and I know you'll take care of her like I can't.'" Willie scratched his head. "Well, shit. We got us a real abandoned baby, here, Ames ol' girl."

"Don't curse in front of her." She shot him an annoyed glare, her left eyebrow inching up her forehead to her hairline.

"It ain't like she can understand me. She's a baby, fer Chri-" Her other eyebrow followed its twin. "*Er,* pity's sake."

"I need something to feed her with." She glanced around her office. "Can you get me one of the cake decorating bottles? The ones with the plastic tip? I think that'll work."

"What'a'ya gonna feed her? Frosting? You ain't got no mother's milk and you can't feed her coffee creamer."

"Dam-I mean, *drat.* You're right. I can give her a little water to hold her over until I can run out and get her some formula."

"Shouldn't you call the police? I mean, she's been abandoned, ain't she? You can't just *keep* her."

Amy shook her head. "First things first. She needs to be fed."

Since it didn't look like Willie was in too much of a hurry to help her, Amy shoved past him and went into the diner's kitchen. From the storage box where she kept her cake-decorating tools, she pulled out a small plastic bottle. Still holding the bawling infant in one hand, she turned on the tap, then let the water run until steam rose from the sink.

"You feeding her boiling water?" Willie asked from behind her. He'd shucked his jacket, ditched the cigarette, and donned his cook's apron. "I don't know nothin' 'bout babies, but even I know *that* ain't right."

Amy rolled her eyes and prayed for patience. "I'm washing this bottle because you're supposed to sterilize things before you give them to an infant. Then I'm going to fill it with warm water to feed her for now."

Willie grunted, then flicked on the grill. "I'll get things set up. You gonna call for back up? You ain't gonna be able to seat and serve with a baby in your arms all day."

Damn. She hadn't considered that. "I'll go call Katie and ask her to come in early. Dottie, too."

Convinced there wasn't a single potential bacteria left alive inside the plastic bottle, Amy filled it with much cooler water. The moment she placed the tip of the bottle into the baby's mouth, the infant started sucking hard, the tops of her tiny cheeks going concave with the effort. Her frustration showed in the amount of squirming her little body did.

A soul-tugging sigh slipped from deep inside Amy. This wasn't going to work for long. The baby needed nourishment and a proper way to get it.

"I'll go make those calls."

After ascertaining both of her most reliable waitresses were on their way, Amy set up the coffee maker one handed, as she propped the decorating bottle against her chin to keep feeding the hungry baby. Then, she emptied the industrial dishwasher, put out place settings on the counter and in the booths, all with one hand.

At five minutes to five and exhausted already, Amy realized Willie spoke the truth. She couldn't work one handed all day, so she placed two additional early morning calls because she needed more than her wait staff's help on this cold Christmas Eve morning.

And she knew exactly the two people she could depend on for it.

Chapter 2

"You have no idea who left her?" Corrine Mills asked as she held the baby in her arms, a baby who sucked vigorously at a real feeding bottle now, filled with formula.

"None." Amy took a whopping gulp from her coffee mug. "It got crazy busy in here yesterday. I don't even remember seeing a customer with an infant. But the note says the mom dined here, so I'm hoping one of the girls remembers her."

As soon as Amy called the two women she regarded as surrogate mothers, they'd come to her rescue, carting a box of much needed baby supplies with them. Powdered formula, bottles, a pacifier, and a package of newborn diapers sat in a box next to Amy, along with a blanket and a few onesie/rompers in newborn sizes. Since all the clothes and the blanket were blue, she knew they belonged to Corrine's grandson, two-year-old Keith.

The three women and the baby were nestled at the back booth closest to Amy's office.

"She must have been in a horrible state to leave her child on a stranger's doorstep. I can't even imagine a level of hopelessness so high," Corrine said. "The maternal instinct to protect one's infant is strong. Unshakably strong. The poor thing must have been at her wit's end and thought she had no other choice. She probably had no one to ask for help."

Amy's thoughts turned to the woman who'd given her life and had subsequently been unable to care for her baby. Left at an orphanage run by Catholic nuns, her mother had never returned and Amy had no information on either of her biological parents. Had the mother who'd abandoned this baby been like her own? Desperate? Overwhelmed?

"Who worked for you yesterday?" Matilda Cudworth asked. "That's a good place to start. Maybe one of the girls remembers her or the baby."

"Or both," Corrine said.

"Dottie worked most of the day. She says she doesn't recall seeing anyone with an infant. Katie and Dani said the same. I haven't been able to get in touch with Racine yet. She left town early this morning to do some last minute mall shopping with her friends. I left a message with her mom to call me when she gets home."

Most of the diner's customers made it a point to stop by and wish the trio a merry Christmas and, Amy knew without a doubt, try to find out why she had a newborn in her arms. Secrets in the tiny town of Dickens were near impossible to keep on the best of days, even for the most hermit-like of the locals. News of a baby popping up in the town's favorite eatery couldn't be contained even if she wanted it to.

No one recognized the infant, or knew of anyone who'd recently given birth, which solidified in Amy's mind the mom hadn't been a local. If she had, someone from the tiny town would have noticed a missing baby.

Corrine put the empty bottle down on the table and lifted the little one to her shoulder. Rubbing her tiny back, she said, "She looks about three weeks, maybe a month old. No more than that. She'll need this diaper changed in a bit," she added, patting the baby's rump. "You didn't find anything about her in the carrier? No name, or any kind of health history?"

"Nope. Which is scary when I think we're giving her generic formula she might be allergic to."

"What do you plan on doing with her?" Matilda asked, smiling when a small, yet thoroughly satisfying, burp blew from the baby. "It's obvious you can't keep her. Have you called anyone yet, aside from us? The police, or social services?"

"No, to both. I hope the mom takes a few hours to think about what she's done and comes to her senses. Hopefully, rational thought will prevail and she'll fly back here to claim her baby. I don't want to get any agencies involved, yet, in case she does."

"Do you think that's wise, Amy?" Corrine asked. "What happens if the mother doesn't return today? It's Christmas tomorrow and I can't imagine child protective services will be able to put her with a foster family, even as an emergency placement, with any kind of ease."

"I'm putting off thinking about it right now," Amy said, rubbing the headache pounding at her temples. "If push comes to shove, I can keep her for a bit. I got my license to be a foster parent in the fall."

"When your parents passed I remember you saying how much you wanted to do that. To give a child a chance like Mike and Delia gave you."

Amy nodded. "I haven't put my name forward yet to take any kids in, though. I wanted to make sure everything ran smoothly with the diner first. But I've got all the necessary certifications. The home visits are all done and I can start whenever I want to."

"Well, you may not be able to wait much longer to notify someone in authority, Amy, because Andy Charles just walked in and he's making a beeline right to our table," Matilda muttered. "And the man doesn't look happy."

The pounding in Amy's head grew louder as the senior Dickens police officer strode straight to them, clad in his uniform, a serious, concerned expression furrowing his usually smooth brow and thinning his mouth. Amy slid from the booth to meet him, toe to toe.

"Amy," he said by way of greeting, and because he'd been raised right, tipped his head to Corrine and Matilda, saying, "Ladies. Happy Holidays." He turned his attention from them immediately back to Amy.

"Hey, Andy," Matilda said, throwing him a smile with more sugar than she usually poured into her sweetened tea. "Why don't you sit down and have a cup of coffee with us? I haven't seen your mother in ages. How's she doing?"

"Fine, ma-am, thanks for asking, but I need to speak to Amy." His intense stare lit back on her. "In an official capacity."

"Somebody told you about the baby." Amy said, tugging her bottom lip under her top teeth.

He fisted his hands on his trim hips and cocked his head to one side, a look of pique filling his handsome face. "Imagine my surprise when Jack Higgins flagged me down and asked if I knew anything about why my girlfriend had a baby at the diner."

"Well, you couldn't have been more surprised hearing about her than I was at finding her," Amy snapped, mimicking his stance and placing her own fists on her hips.

"My surprise is because you weren't the one told me, Amy. Or anyone in the police department for that matter, about a baby you found at your back door."

"It all happened so fast, I haven't had a chance to report it yet."

His eyes narrowed as he turned and raked a glance over the two women sitting in the booth, then back to her, his thoughts apparent.

Blushing to the roots of her hair, Amy shook her head. "The baby was hungry, Andy, and my first and only consideration was to feed her. I knew Corrine and Matilda could help me."

His gaze slid to the empty bottle sitting next to Corrine's coffee mug, then pulled back to her. "Mission accomplished."

Her own eyes squinted now and she channeled her dear departed adoptive mother for the strength to keep unsaid the words she wanted to let fly.

Taking a mental breath, she pulled deep for calm. "Why don't we go into my office and discuss this in private?" Before he could say anything else, she nodded at the women, said, "I'll be right back," and then strode through the swing door leading down a quick hallway to her office.

Once through it, she took another breath – a physical one this time – before she turned around to face the man she'd been involved, and fancied herself in love with, for almost a year.

"I know that look like the back of my hand," Andy said. He shook his head as he closed the door behind him. "It usually means there's a come to Jesus lecture about to be spoken and I should bow my head and fold my hands."

When a corner of his kissable mouth lifted, her annoyance fled. Andy took two steps forward, his arms outstretched and she went into them willingly and without hesitation.

As she breathed in the scent of leather from his uniform jacket, Amy closed her eyes.

"Sweetheart, why didn't you call me right away? You know I would have been here in a blink, sirens blaring if I had to."

She pulled back, quirked an eyebrow and asked, "And this would be because you carry formula and diapers in your patrol car, would it?"

He had the grace to look sheepish. "Well, no. But I could have run out and gotten them for you."

It took her a millisecond to realize he wasn't so much angry as hurt he hadn't been her first call. She cuddled into him again.

"The only reason I called Corrine and Matilda is because I wanted to talk to my mom. Unfortunately, I couldn't." His arms tightened around her waist. "Since those two are like mothers to me, I called them." She shifted so she could look into his eyes. "I figured they'd know what to do, what I'd need. And they did. That's all it was." She cupped his cheeks and placed a sweet kiss on his mouth.

He sighed against her lips. "It's a good thing your door is closed because if anyone saw me kissing you while I'm on duty, I'd never hear the end of it from the Chief."

She kissed the tip of his nose and then pulled out of his embrace.

"I need to call CPS, Amy, to report the baby. You know that. What if she's been stolen and the real mother is out there looking frantically for her?"

"I don't think so. Why would the person who stole her leave her here? That makes no sense."

Andy shrugged. "Regardless, the baby's been abandoned and there are legal protocols that need to implemented."

"Just give me a little time, please, before we inform some state agency about the baby. I'm hoping the mom will come back. I'd hate to drag her into the system, because it's apparent she's having difficulty as it is."

Andy shook his head. "You're putting me in a tough position, sweetheart. If the Chief hears about this and finds out I didn't report an abandoned baby right away, it could come down hard on me."

"Can't you pretend you don't know?"

He nailed her with an are-you-kidding-me glare.

"Guess not." She gnawed on her inner cheek.

"Let's do this," he said a moment later. "Come back outside with me and I can interview you. That will at least make it seem like I did something official if I'm asked. I can keep the interview open and not file it if the mom comes back."

Her smile bloomed fast and full. She leaned in and kissed his mouth, this time, taking her time about it.

Andy broke free first. When he pulled back, his expression mimicked the one he usually had when she slipped in a piece of pie with his lunch order. Eyes soft and misty, the corners of his mouth tipped into a boyish smirk.

"Thank you," she said.

"Don't thank me yet. If the mom hasn't returned by the end of my shift, I'll need to file the report. Understand?"

She nodded.

"Good, now, let's go sit down and make a show of this to your customers."

"All good?" Matilda asked when they emerged from Amy's office.

"Yuppers," she said.

"So, what can you tell me?" Andy began as he sat next to Corrine, who still held the baby. He glanced at the small bundle in the older woman's arms.

"She sure is a cutie pie," he said before Amy could begin.

"That she is. And I imagine her mama's at her wit's end to force her to do something like abandon her," Corrine said.

"You talk like you know the mom," Andy said, his eyes drifting up to the older woman. "Do you have any idea whose baby this is?"

"Not a one," the older woman assured him. "I don't even know anyone who's pregnant right now or who has given birth in the past month."

He peered at her for a moment before he shifted to Matilda.

"Ditto," she said before he uttered a word. "And I haven't seen anyone new with a baby come into the store lately. Maybe Doc Martin knows someone."

Andy nodded. "Not a bad idea to ask him. Okay. So, Amy, take me through the events of this morning."

His slip into his official voice had her toes curling. Andy Charles was without doubt the sexiest man she'd ever dated and the fact he didn't even know it made him even more so.

Taking a breath, she related how she'd found the baby, the calls to the two women and her waitresses, and the note pinned in the baby carrier. When he asked, she pulled it from her pocket and handed it over.

"From the words in this note, mom and baby were in here yesterday."

"Yes, but I never saw them. Neither did Dottie. I called Racine Edmonds to ask her, but she's out shopping."

"Do you still have yesterday's receipts or have you gone to the bank yet?"

She tossed him an are-you-kidding head tilt and eye roll, to which he replied, nervously, "No, of course not. You've been...preoccupied. Well, we can run through the receipts and try to find a credit card for this girl."

"She wouldn't have paid with a card," Corrine said as she rocked the sleeping infant. "She'd want to keep a low profile, make it difficult to identify her if she'd planned on leaving her baby."

"That makes sense," Matilda chimed in.

Andy nodded. "You're probably right. Did the baby have anything with her to indicate who she is? A monogramed blanket, maybe?"

"Generic store-bought," Amy said. "The note's the only thing she had with her. Like I said, no diapers, no formula. Basically, just a crying baby in a carrier."

"Which is where we came in," Matilda said.

"Amy?" Dottie called from the counter, holding the receiver of the wall phone. "Racine's on the line for you."

"Be right back," she told them. "Hey, Rae," she said into the phone. "Got a question for you. Do remember a customer yesterday, maybe a youngish girl, with an infant?"

When the waitress replied she did, and then volunteered some information, Amy told her to hang on and then motioned Andy over.

"I'm going to give you to Officer Charles, Rae. He's got a few questions for you."

She handed the phone off, then went back to the table.

"She remembers the mom," she told her two friends, accepting the baby from Corrine. Settled back in the booth with the tiny, sleeping, and now blessedly quiet infant nestled against her, Amy added, "Thinks she was in her mid-to-late twenties. Came in with the baby in a carrier during lunch, sat in a booth and ordered just a coke and toast. Paid in cash," she added, looking at Corrine. "Racine said she looked bone tired, the bags under her eyes like suitcases."

"I remember those first few sleep deprived months," Matilda said. "One morning I put coffee grounds in the blender instead of the Mr. Coffee, then couldn't figure out why my brew tasted like hot water."

Corrine nodded. "Once, I went to the market in my pajama bottoms and slippers, thinking I was fully dressed." She grinned at Amy. "It was the dead of winter and I didn't even feel the cold because I was a walking zombie from the lack of sleep."

Corrine tilted her head as she gazed at Amy. "Babies are a huge responsibility and take up all your time."

"I know."

"Teething and fussiness. Constant diaper changes. Formula issues causing tummy upsets."

"Diaper rash. Baby proofing the house. Not to mention you can't simply up and leave to run to the store. You need to bring enough with you for any emergency that could pop up," Matilda said, "or have a sitter on call twenty four hours a day."

"You can never go anywhere without the baby if you don't have a sitter. " Corrine bobbed her head a few times. "Grocery shopping with a teething, crying infant is one of the nine circles of Hell. You can't take a shower because you need to hear if the baby cries. Quick sink baths were all I managed for almost a year unless my husband was home. And even then I had to be fast because he'd let me know if the baby was crying and have me deal with it. It's a different time now. Fathers are more involved with day-to-day care than when our kids were small."

They all glanced at the baby.

"Speaking of that, I wonder where her daddy is?" Corrine asked.

"Maybe he doesn't know about her?" Matilda said. "Or if he does, he might not know the mama did what she did."

Amy's head ping-ponged between them while they rattled on. "You two make motherhood sound like it's not for the faint-hearted. It's a wonder anyone has kids."

With a smile, Matilda rubbed her finger across the baby's cheek. "It isn't a picnic in the park, for sure. But the reward, when all is said and done, is you're gifted with a precious little angel like this one."

All three women smiled down at the sleeping baby.

"Okay," Andy said coming back to the table, his notebook in his hand. "Racine would make a good cop. She remembered a ton of stuff about the mom. Didn't get her name, though, but her description is good."

"What are you going to do?" Amy asked, cuddling the infant closer, lest he try to pry it from her arms.

"What we discussed in your office."

She let out a silent sigh of relief.

"I might have Deke Acres do a drawing of the mom based on Racine's description. But if the mom isn't back here by the time I get off shift, I'm gonna have to notify child protective services."

His eyes turned soft like they had in her office as he watched Amy gently rock the baby. "You're a natural, Ames."

Corrine beamed at him. "I was just thinking the same thing," she said, a twinkle shining in her eyes. It didn't escape Amy's notice his neck flushed at the older woman's intense perusal.

"Just imagine the beautiful babies Amy will have...someday," Matilda said, sending him a similar smile.

Amy knew the poor man would probably blush himself into a sweat if she didn't intervene.

"Okay, Andy," she said, drawing his embarrassed attention back to her. "I'll let you know if she shows up. You go keep the citizens of Dickens safe."

With a crooked lift to his lips, he tapped an imaginary cap to the three of them and told her, "I'll be in touch."

"You know," Matilda said once he'd gone, "Christmas is a lovely time to get engaged."

"And married, too," Corrine added. "I got married on December 26th, a picture perfect New England winter's day."

"Cold, dreary, and overcast?" Amy said, trying hard—and failing—to hide her smirk. More than once since she'd started dating Andy, these two self-professed godmothers had slung hints and wedding suggestion dates her way. While she could take it in stride, knowing her mother would be doing the same thing if she were alive, she could sense Andy was more the let's-take-it-slow kind of man, which suited her just fine. She had more than enough on her proverbial plate with running the business her parents left in her care. Adding a fiancé, and all the implied planning-a-wedding stuff it entailed, was something she didn't mind putting off a bit.

Yes, she'd passed through the door into her thirties a few months ago and if she wanted children – which she did – she knew she needed to start working on producing some before her eggs turned to powder.

Was Andy the man she wanted to make those babies with?

Something to think about later when she didn't have another woman's baby in her arms, a baby who'd gone crimson faced and fidgety, its little legs pulling up, then straightening.

"Someone's gearing for a blow-out," Matilda said.

"There's diapers and wipes in the bag," Corrine told her, pointing. "Enough for today, anyway."

A loud *splat* followed by an odor remarkably similar to rotten eggs wafted from the baby's bottom half a second later.

"Oh, good God," Amy cried when the smell flew up her nose. Rising from the booth, she told the women, "I'd better change her before someone calls the health department about a noxious odor and gets me closed down for an inspection."

She carried the sound of their laughter with her to her office.

Chapter 3

"The rush is finally over," Dottie said as she wiped down the counter. "I swear, I've never seen so many last minute shoppers before this year. And every one of them felt compelled to stop for a bite to eat before heading home. You'd think people would want to be snuggled up in their own houses, relaxing on Christmas Eve. Or at least home wrapping gifts and cooking."

Amy suspected part of the reason they'd had so many customers had much to do with the baby in her arms.

All morning long people she never saw except to say hello to on the street, in church, or in the grocery store found the time to stop by for a cup of coffee, strike up a conversation, and get a gander at the baby. Some of them offered her supplies like extra diapers and bottles if she needed it. A few volunteered to take the baby so Amy could work for a few minutes and use both hands. Even Doc Martin, one of the town's favorite family practice physicians stopped by, supposedly on his way to visit a patient at Dickens Memorial. He'd held the infant, agreed based on size and development she was about a month old, and had then done a quick reflex check before pronouncing her healthy and apparently well cared for.

When asked, he claimed none of his patients had given birth in the past two months, although a few were ready to go in the next few days,

He hadn't debated Amy's decision not to call child protective services yet, even though he was obligated to report the baby, because he agreed with her assessment the mom would probably come back as soon as she realized what she'd done.

"It wouldn't be the first time I've seen it happen," he said as he shrugged back into his overcoat while in her office. "It can all be so debilitating and overwhelming for a new mother, especially a first baby, if that's what this little one is. Hormones are raging. Sleep is a commodity worth its weight in gold." He shook his head. "It does no good reporting the mom and getting state agencies involved if it can be handled with a little compassion and understanding."

Thoughts of her own biological mother flooded Amy's mind again. Had there been no one in her life to offer compassion and understanding during the time after her child's birth? Is that why she'd left her daughter in the care of the nuns? She'd had no support system? No one to guide her, help her, or even offer her a lifeline?

"Let me know if you need anything, or if the baby does," Doc Martin told her. "I'm on call over the holiday and I expect I'm going to be delivering at least two babies." He chuckled. "It's a race to see which will be the first Christmas arrival of the season in Dickens and win a sleigh full of baby stuff from the Chamber of Commerce."

The diner stood empty now except for a lone trucker who'd stopped for a break from the road and a burger to fill him up for the long haul home. Since winter had officially arrived on the calendar, darkness now descended on the town by four in the afternoon, with snow predicted tonight. By Christmas morning the town could be blanketed in anywhere from four to eight inches of the white stuff depending on which way the wind decided to shift during the wee hours.

Amy leaned a hip against the counter. The baby in her arms was sucking on her fourth bottle of the day.

"I never knew babies ate so much," Dottie said, ticking her head toward the infant. "Seems like every time I've turned around today I've seen you feeding her, changing her, or burping her."

"Little tummies fill up fast," Amy responded. Then she rolled her eyes and added, "And empty just as quick."

Dottie shuddered. "Which is why you'll never see me having one," the twenty-two year old said. "I've got things I want to do with my life and being tied down with a baby isn't one of them."

Amy kept her opinion the girl might change her mind in the future to herself.

Just as the baby finished, Amy spotted Andy's squad car pull into the parking lot.

"I'm heading back to my office for a bit," she told Dottie. She wanted privacy for the conversation she was about to have with the good officer.

The baby fell back to sleep after burping, so Amy settled her into her infant carrier, the blanket nestled around her tiny form.

"Dottie said you were back here," Andy said from the doorway, seconds later.

She turned, nodded, and then took a bracing breath.

"The mom never showed."

"I figured since"—he pointed to where the carrier sat on her desk—"she's still here. Listen, I informed the Chief about the baby after I spoke to Racine. I felt I had to."

She hissed in a breath. "What did he say?"

"Surprisingly, he's of the same mindset as Corrine and Matilda. With the holiday being tomorrow, placing her with a family is going to be tough. He did tell me, though, to keep him apprised of the situation and if the mom didn't show, we'd need to do something."

She didn't like the baby being referred to as a *situation*, but at least the Chief hadn't reported her to social services.

Yet.

"Listen," Amy said, crossing to Andy and then taking one of his hands in hers. She gave it a squeeze. "It's Christmas Eve and I know we planned on spending it together."

He quirked an eyebrow. "And I hope we still are."

She beamed at him. "Of course. I've got a chicken cooking upstairs in the crock pot and a bottle of wine in the fridge."

"I do love your slow cooked chicken." The warm expression in his eyes sent a tingle of anticipation up her spine.

"That's why I made it. But, it's Christmas Eve, like I said, and since most agencies have probably already closed for the holiday—"

"Amy—"

"Hear me out, please?"

He shook his head, then, let out a slow breath. "Even though I know what you're going to say, go ahead."

She took a step closer, the hand she held now cocooned in both of hers. She lifted it to her torso, and stared him straight in the eyes. "We can go ahead and call CPS if it's absolutely necessary—"

"It is."

She blinked a few times. "Okay. But I want to be the one to foster her over the holiday. Maybe longer if the mom can't be located."

"Amy—"

"I've got my license," she steamrolled right over him, "already finished all my home visits. I've just been waiting for the right time."

"And you think Christmas is that time?"

"What better day? This little one"—she thrust her chin over her shoulder at the infant—"has been abandoned. *On Christmas Eve.* She has no way to fend for herself."

"Of course not. She's a baby, Amy."

She flashed him another smile.

"It makes sense she stay here with me, since I've already had her for the day. We've gotten into a kind of...routine."

"Social services might not agree, especially when they find out you didn't call them the moment you found her."

In truth, she hadn't considered they wouldn't. But a caseworker might not take kindly to the fact she'd waited so long to notify the authorities.

"But like every one has said, it's a holiday and emergency placement will be difficult at best. I've already established a bond with her and have been taking care of her for hours." She turned her head again to the sleeping baby then back to him. "She's comfortable, fed, warm, has a clean diaper, and right now seems utterly content."

Andy shook his head and dropped his chin to his chest. When he lifted his gaze back to zero in on Amy, she could tell he wasn't on board with her idea the way she'd hoped he'd be. "All babies are utterly content when they're sleeping." He blew out a breath

"What's wrong?"

"I have to ask, Amy, if you're thinking with your head right now, or your heart?"

"I'll like to think both."

"I'm not sure I agree. I think your emotions are guiding you more, and you're not considering what's really going on."

Stunned into silence, she gaped at him.

He took a step closer and squeezed the hand he held. "I think you're looking at this little one, seeing a parallel to your own life, and it's directing your decisions."

"I was left at an orphanage, Andy, not the back door of a diner."

"True, but isn't the end result the same?" When she didn't answer him, he said, "You were both abandoned."

She couldn't debate his point because it was the simple truth.

"I don't think," he added, "you've really considered the logistics of what fostering this baby will look like."

"What do you mean?"

"Well, for one thing, do you have a crib? Or a bassinette? You've got a few emergency supplies that helped get you through the day, but do you have a stock of diapers? Bottles? Formula? Tomorrow's, like you've said, Christmas. All the stores will be closed and you won't have a way to run out and get her what she needs. What about an emergency kit with one of those"—he swiped a finger in the air—"nasal suction things, in case she gets sick? Have you got a plan in place for who's going to watch her when you're downstairs at the diner if you keep her longer than just a few days? Have you considered any of those things?"

Her happiness began to fade at each item he ticked off.

"Babies have erratic sleep schedules, up every couple hours to be fed and changed," Andy continued. "How will you manage the diner and still be able to function and care for the baby without feeling like a zombie? You work fourteen hour days, seven days a week as it is."

Had she gotten caught up in the emotion of the situation? Seen too many parallels to her own life?

One of the main reasons she'd dreamed of becoming a foster parent was so she could help make a scary time in a child's life better. To offer comfort, shelter, and love, when the child so desperately needed it.

But every time she'd imagined having a foster child, it *had* been a child. Not a baby.

Was there really a difference? Both a child and an infant needed love, care, and support in the absence of a parent. Both were hard work, to be sure, but the end result of knowing you'd made a difference in a little one's life was so worthwhile.

"The mom left her here, but what about the baby's father, or grandparents? They're probably searching for her, frantic because she's missing," Andy said.

"Maybe not," Amy said. "The note said the mom had no way to care for a baby by herself, which tells me the dad isn't in the picture and the mom has no one to lean on, like parents."

He stared at her for a moment before releasing a sigh. "I did a run on missing persons reports today, looking to see if anyone reported a missing baby."

Ice ran through her veins. "And?"

He shrugged. "Nothing hit, but it could merely be the grandparents or the father don't know the baby's missing yet. There are so many variables here, Amy, it's enough to make my head spin."

Delia Dorrit always claimed her adopted daughter possessed a backbone forged in iron, so Amy steeled her spine, stood straight, and looked Andy right in the eyes, conviction in her voice when she said, "Well, until the father or her grandparents come looking for her, the baby has to stay somewhere and it might as well be here. I can improvise a crib for her tonight with a dresser drawer and some towels to cushion underneath and around her. When the stores are open again I can get her an inexpensive portable crib. Corrine, knowing how much babies need to be changed, dropped off an entire box of diapers this afternoon along with a case of formula after every thing she already brought me this morning. Matilda dropped of two boxes of infant clothes she had stored at her house for when her daughters bring their kids for sleepovers. And if I asked, she'd probably lend me her spare crib. Doc Martin left me an emergency kit, and yes, it does have a nasal suction bulb in it."

She took a step back from him, turned, and rubbed a hand over the blanket. "As far as work is concerned, tomorrow the diner is closed. Willie will be back on the twenty-sixth," she held up an index finger to him, halting what he'd been about to say.

He closed his mouth.

"As will Dottie and Racine," she went on. "My best staff. And the day after the holiday is usually the slowest one of the year. That'll give me another day to figure something out if she's still here."

He shook his head again and parked his hands on his hips. "So you've given this some thought, I see."

"Of course I have."

He nodded. "Okay. Everything you've said is good for the baby, Amy, but what about us? Where does you taking this baby in, leave us?"

"Us?"

"Yeah." He moved closer and slid both of his hands into hers now. "We have so little time together as it is with your work hours and my shift schedule. Some weeks we barely manage more than a few hours of alone time. With you fostering a baby, who will take up all your time – free and not—there won't be much left for me. For us." He shook his head. "And I hear how selfish I sound. Here you are, willing to upset your life, turn it on its ear, to take care of a baby who isn't even your own. I could love you for that alone, Amy, if I wasn't already so stupid in love with you for a million other reasons."

She let go of his hands, wound them around his waist and melted into him. Andy had been the first to say 'I love you' months ago, way before she'd made the decision to welcome him into her bed, a decision she hadn't made lightly. In such a small town, gossipy tongues wagged freely and reputations could be ruined with one salacious verbal swipe. Since they were both in the public eye, they'd taken measures to try and keep the details of their relationship as quiet as possible. But, because Dickens *was* a quintessential small town, everybody knew they were an item.

And, as luck would have it, everyone approved.

Andy Charles was well respected and liked by the community he served and most expected him to be elevated to police chief once the current chief retired. They'd have even less time together when that happened.

"I don't want to lose you, Amy. Lose us. Lose what we have together."

"We won't." She pressed against his jacket. "We'll make it work. I promise. Couples with a new baby do it every day, many with a lot less support than we have."

His hands tightened around her waist. After a moment he pulled back and stared down at her. He didn't look altogether convinced, but when he nodded and said, "Okay. Let me make a call," she breathed a sigh of relief.

While he did, Amy went back into the diner, turned the open sign to closed, locked the door, then told Dottie to stop sweeping and get on home. In the kitchen she found Willie wiping down the grill.

"Almost done," he told her. "Everything's cleaned up, put away and ready to go when we open again on the twenty-sixth. Tomorrow you can sleep in and not worry about this place."

"I think I worry about it even in my sleep," she said, with a chuckle as she looked for something to help with or straighten. As usual, she found nothing. Willie may look and act like an ornery, wizened biker with his waist length, gray, ponytail, four days of scruff on his chin, and tattoos circling his biceps, but she'd never known a more meticulous person when it came to keeping a work space organized and tidy.

"Yeah, I expect you do. How's the little one doing?"

"Fed and sleeping. Again."

His deep, cigarette-raspy chuckle pulled a smile from her.

"Sounds like a plan I can get in front of."

"What are you doing tomorrow?" she asked. "Sleeping in, too?"

He nodded. "That. Then I've got...plans."

Her grin widened. "And do those plans concern a certain red haired siren whose name begins with an R and ends with UBY, and who makes the best pies in three states?"

His laugh brought on a croak-filled coughing spasm. "It does," he said, swiping at the tears moistening his eyes, post-cough. "It'll just be the two of us, 'cuz her kids are in Florida visiting their father." He untied his apron and hung it, and his cap, on the peg by the kitchen door. "If you don't need me for anything else, I'm headin' out. I need to get one more present, then get on home."

As she had every Christmas Eve since she'd turned seven and he'd come to work for her parents, Amy lifted up on her toes, kissed his cheek and said, "Merry Christmas."

"And to you, Ames. Tell Andy I wish him the same."

"Will do."

Amy shut the lights in the restaurant proper, then the kitchen, and made her way back to her office to find Andy hanging up her desk phone.

"Took me a few minutes to get connected to Child Protective Services, but they're sending someone right over. Turns out, there's a social worker in town today taking care of another emergency placement. A kid over at Dickens Memorial. She's finishing up there and then heading straight here."

A tiny stab of anxiety pierced Amy's soul. "I'll go get my license and certification. I've got everything upstairs in my apartment."

He stopped her by taking her hands. "Notifying them is the right thing to do, Amy."

"I know. I know. I'm just a little...nervous, I guess." She turned around to glance at the still sleeping baby. "After all this, I might not be granted emergency custody."

He gently kissed her, then let his lips drift up her cheek. "I have a feeling that's not going to happen." He sighed. "I'm officially off duty now, so I'll stay, meet this social worker with you. Okay? I can be a kind of reinforcement. Which you don't need," he added, a corner of his mouth tipping upward, "but still."

"It's more than okay," she told him. The kindness and love shining in his eyes went a long way in the dissolution of her apprehension.

"Let me go get my paperwork."

Chapter 4

Jane Barker looked exactly like what Amy imagined an overworked and underpaid social worker would. The tall and imposing fiftyish woman with salt and pepper colored, tight curls cropped close to her head, wore a pair of reading glasses on a chain secured around her neck. Three weeks of needed sleep wouldn't eradicate the eggplant colored smudges under her eyes. A dark, ill-fitting pantsuit hung from her bony frame and Amy's first thought upon shaking her hand was to offer her something warm and nutritious to eat from the diner menu.

Her steely grey eyes raked Amy's apartment when she entered, terrifying Amy that she'd find the space lacking in the needed environment for the baby. Amy snuck a quick, worried side-glance at Andy, who shook his head and mouthed *relax*.

Impossible she mouthed back.

Before saying a word, Mrs. Barker zeroed in on the infant carrier settled next to the living room couch, and her entire demeanor changed. A beatific smile bloomed on her thin lips as she lifted the sleeping baby into her arms and cuddled her securely against her chest, cooing gently to her.

While holding her, the social worker asked for a tour of Amy's apartment, then grilled her on the events of the day. Andy provided backup with the telling, explaining how they'd hoped the mother would return.

Mrs. Barker sighed. "That's always the hope," she said, placing the baby back in the carrier. "Let's sit down." She motioned to the kitchen table, set for the dinner Amy had prepared.

"First, you have to know you should have notified the agency right away when you discovered the baby. Precious time has been lost in locating the mother because we weren't made aware of the situation."

Amy's stomach fell to the floor.

"Having said that, I understand why you didn't. Your first thought to feed her and make sure she was safe and out of any danger was the correct one, and it's commendable in a foster parent, since your first obligation is to the welfare of the child under your care."

Nodding, Amy took a full breath.

"Your paperwork is all in order, Miss Dorrit," Mrs. Barker said, referring to a large portfolio she removed from her worn and stuffed briefcase. "Your application to foster is on file and current, and your license is valid." She looked over the top rims of her glasses at Amy. "I do have a few concerns, though, about leaving the infant in your care."

Amy swallowed again, hope fleeting once more. "Okay," she managed to eek out.

"First, you've never fostered before and a baby is much different from taking a child in. She will require twenty-four hour care. Not that a child wouldn't, but infants are different. You run your own business. While that's commendable for a woman of your age, how do you plan on caring for a baby when you have to oversee the diner? You are a single woman without any kind of ancillary help, be it from a husband, or a parent of your own. You live alone."

Amy took a breath, then calmly told her about all the support systems she had in place, naming Corrine, Matilda, even Doc Martin. Andy piped in, adding himself into the mix.

"I may not be her husband," he said, glancing at Amy, "but I'm more than willing to pitch in and give her a hand."

She thanked him with her eyes, then told the social worker, "My staff is a highly capable group and I have no problem with them working without me looking over their shoulders. Besides, the week after Christmas is one of our slowest of the year and I typically cut our hours of operation by a third until after the New Year."

"So that's one week you've got covered. What about more?"

"Excuse me?"

"What if the child requires long term fostering? If the mother, father, or a grandparent, doesn't show up to claim her? Are you able to commit to the long term care this baby will need?"

In truth, Amy hadn't gotten farther than the New Year in her thinking.

"I can see it hasn't occurred to you," Mrs. Barker said, not unkindly, as she removed her glasses and peered across the table at Amy. "I have no difficulty granting emergency custody to you since this is a holiday. In truth, you've made my job a lot easier because I don't have to locate someone to take her in on such short notice. But, if this turns out to be a long term foster situation, I need to know if you're prepared to give her up to a family who can offer her the care she needs without worrying about outside forces."

Was she? Amy hadn't thought about or considered anything permanent, but now that the question was posed, she saw it as a possibility.

"I'll let you think about it over the holiday," Mrs. Barker said, closing her portfolio. "For now, I'm granting you emergency guardianship. I'll file the paperwork with the court and I'll be back on the twenty-sixth to evaluate how everything is going and to update you on whether or not her family has been located."

Before leaving she handed Amy her business card, wished her good luck, and a Merry Christmas.

"*Oh, my God.*" Amy fell back against the door after she closed it. "I thought, for sure, she was going to leave with the baby."

Andy pulled her into his arms and kissed her temple. "Like she said, you made her job easier. But don't think she'll make anything easy for you. Her concerns are valid."

"I know." She nuzzled her nose against his uniform. "Let's get through the next few days. I'm still hopeful the mom will surface and claim her."

"I really like you included me in that sentence," he said as he rubbed her back.

She pulled back and stared up at his warm eyes. With a smile she said, "Always," then kissed him.

The baby's loud wake-up wail broke the moment and had them both pulling back, laughing.

"I guess this is a good peak into what life with a new baby is like," he said, shaking his head, his smile going lopsided.

After she'd been fed, changed and then placed back in her carrier with a pacifier courtesy of Matilda, Amy served dinner while the baby sucked away.

"What should we call her?" Andy asked, pouring some wine into their glasses, and thrusting his chin at the baby. The sound of the infant's sucking rang out, loud and wet, in the room and her round eyes were glassy. "We can't keep referring to her as *the baby*, can we?"

"Do you think it's right we give her a name since she has one already?"

"The mom didn't divulge it, which was a smart move on her part because in the eyes of the law she's merely Baby Jane Doe. If she'd given us a name we could make it public with a plea for the mom or dad to come forward. Since you're caring for her, I think it makes sense you get to call her whatever you want."

Amy let her mind run rampant as she ate her salad. When a small grin began to cross her face, Andy cocked his head. "That's a wicked smile, Amy Dorrit. What are you thinking?"

"Well," she said, leaning her elbows on the table as she tossed a quick glance once again at the baby, "It's Christmas. I guess we could be schmaltzy and call her Noel, or Kris. Maybe even Merry."

"What about Angel? Carol? Eve?"

Laughing, she added, "Grace, Joy or Hope?"

"I like Holly. Or Star."

"Why not Winter? Or Ivy?"

Andy nodded. "Cute."

"They're all cute, but I don't think she looks like any of them."

"Can a baby really look like a name?"

She shrugged. "I want to call her something else. Something you don't hear all the time."

"Such as?"

"Promise me you won't laugh."

"I'd never laugh at you, Amy. You know that."

"Remember those words after I tell you what I want to call her and why."

He tilted his head as he regarded her through those eyes she loved looking into. "Now I'm intrigued."

She bit down on the inside of her cheek. After taking a bracing breath, she said, "Well, since she just kind of...appeared," she flipped her hand in the air, "like a puff of smoke in a magic act, how about Abra?"

His head tilt became more pronounced. "Come again?"

"Abra. You know? Like in *abracadabra.*" She waved both hands in the air now, as if brandishing a wand and making something disappear.

He blinked a few times, then shook his head. "For real?"

She nodded. "I like it. It's...unusual and unique."

"Those are two words for it. I can think of a bunch more."

With a pout, she said, "Don't be mean. We can call her Abra, for short. I'm sure if I looked it up the name would mean something."

"Yeah, like *'make me disappear'* in old Phoenician."

She tossed him a haughty, one-eyed squint, then forked in more of her salad. After swallowing she pointed the utensil at him. "I'm calling her Abra. Deal with it."

His grin started slow, tugging at the corners of his kissable lips first until it began to steadily spread wider. When the twin dimples crevassing his cheeks popped up, Amy sighed. And when he stretched a hand across the table and she slid one of her own into it, those little flutters that always batted about in her tummy at his touch went into overdrive.

"Abra it is," he said.

After they finished dinner, they cuddled on Amy's couch in front of the lit tree, an old Dean Martin Christmas album of her mother's playing in the background on the stereo.

With her head nestled on the shoulder of the man she loved, and with one hand gently rubbing the top of the blanket covering the sleeping baby in her carrier, Amy was hard pressed to ever remember a more contented moment. Snow started falling during dinner, ensuring a white Christmas morning. A brisk wind echoed through the bare treetops outside. It crossed her mind all they needed for a picture perfect holiday scene was a roaring fire.

"Wish we had a fire right now," Andy said aloud.

"You're a mind reader." She shifted and kissed his jaw. "Want to open your present?"

He kissed the tip of her nose. "Where's the fun in that? Don't you want to wait until Christmas morning, get up and run to the tree to see what Santa brought you?"

"No."

He laughed and chucked her chin. "Too bad. I want to wait till morning. Half the fun is the expectation."

"That leaves the other half as frustration at not knowing what you're going to get."

"How old are you?" He shook his head.

"Not so old I still don't love getting presents."

"And I love seeing you open them." He kissed her nose again. "In the morning."

She tossed him another pout. It instantly fled when the baby sighed and cooed next to them, her eyes flickering behind her eyelids. They both turned their attention to the little bundle.

"What do you think she's dreaming about?" Amy asked.

"A full tummy and a clean diaper, I'd imagine. What else does she know?"

Laughing, Amy squeezed his arm. "Well, that's true." Shifting, she sat up straight and stretched. "Maybe we should head to bed, get some rest? We've got about an hour or so before Abra wakes up again to be fed and I'd like to get a little shut eye before I'm totally sleep deprived."

Minutes later, with the bottom drawer of Amy's dresser situated on the floor next to the bed and draped in towels and a fleece blanket, Amy shut the light and crawled in next to Andy. He pulled her into his arms and covered them with the comforter.

"I'll take first feeding shift," he whispered. "You get some sleep."

As her eyes drifted closed, she whispered back, "You're the best present I've ever gotten."

She fell asleep to the sound of his deep chuckle.

Chapter 5

The warmth of the bright sunshine filtering through her bedroom curtains stirred Amy. The last time she'd woken to daylight had been exactly 365 days ago on the previous Christmas morning. The desire to close her eyes again and fall back to sleep seeped through her.

The memory of why she couldn't shot to the front of her mind a moment later.

A quick pat of the bed next to her told her she was alone. A glance over the side showed her an empty makeshift crib.

She found her man in her grandmother's rocking chair, Abra in his arms as he held a bottle for her. The only sound in the quiet room was the baby sucking. He'd made coffee, a steaming cup of it next to him on the end table, just within reach.

Amy's heart swelled. The sight of Andy, clad in a t-shirt and sweat pants, his hair a riot of spikes and whirls and with a sheet mark slashed across one cheek, sitting in her rocking chair cooing to a feeding baby brought tears of boundless love and joy to her eyes.

She must have made a sound, because he lifted his head to find her standing in the doorway.

"Merry Christmas," he whispered, a crooked smile on his sleepy face. "She woke up a few minutes ago and since I know you get this one morning a year to sleep late, I figured I'd get her fed and changed so you could catch a few more hours. Get back into bed. I've got her."

With determination in her step and love billowing through her, she crossed the room, cradled the baby's head in her hand, and bent to kiss the man she loved.

"Merry Christmas," she whispered against his lips. "I love you."

His lazy smile took its time spreading across his face.

"I'm surprised you're awake. She got you up twice during the night."

"She got you up, too." She lifted a shoulder under her robe. "Like you told me yesterday, babies have erratic sleep schedules. At least after a bottle and a diaper change, she went back down easily. No fussing. No crying. From everything Corrine and Matilda told me yesterday, that's a gift. Let me have her."

"Here. She's almost done." They switched positions with Amy now seated in the chair, Andy kneeling in front of them.

"Speaking of gifts," he said, "Santa came."

Amy rolled her tired eyes and shook her head at him.

"Want to see what he brought you?" His eyebrows wiggled up and down, playfully.

She glanced over her shoulder. "I don't see anything under the tree but your present," she told him. "Where did...*Santa,* leave mine?"

"Right here." He slipped a hand into the pocket of his sweats and pulled out a small box tied with a red ribbon. "I told him I'd hold on to it until you woke up."

Amy stared down at the box, her heart deciding to start dancing to a disco beat, her legs following suit and bouncing up and down nervously. The baby jolted in her arms, but continued to drink.

"What—what is that?" Her voice shook as much as the rest of her body.

"Your Christmas present," Andy said, simply, adding, "but before you can open it I need to say something."

It was at that moment she realized he'd wasn't kneeling on both legs next to her, but with only one bent, the hand holding the box resting against his thigh.

"Andy?"

"Let me talk, now, Amy. You sit and feed Abra while I say this, okay?"

Her "okay" came out like a frog's morning croak.

Andy took a deep breath, held it for a moment, then slowly let it out, his lips lifting into a warm smile as he gazed at her.

"It's no secret I love you, Amy. I have since the first time I came into the diner for lunch and you asked me what kind of pie I liked."

"Key Lime," she said, without a thought.

He nodded. "Right away you pulled a huge slice out from under the pie dome and gave it to me, on the house because, you declared, I had excellent taste in pies."

"You do."

"I have excellent taste in women, too," he said. "In one woman in particular." He cleared his throat, then popped open the box in his hand.

When Amy gasped, the baby startled again. This time, though, she started to fuss.

"It's okay, sweetheart," Amy cooed as she stared, wide eyed at the beautiful emerald cut diamond housed in the box.

"This was my grandmother's engagement ring," Andy told her. "She gave it to me before she died with a promise to only ever give it to the woman I wanted to spend my life with. You're that woman, Amy. I know your life is a little turned sideways right now with the baby and running the diner, and the million other things you do on a daily basis, but I've been thinking about asking you to marry me for the longest time. I'd planned on doing this last night, but with Abra, I figured I'd take a back seat until this morning."

That statement alone would have prompted her to say yes if she'd been anywhere on the fence about marrying him.

But she wasn't.

She'd been in love with Andy Charles almost as long as he claimed to be with her. But she hadn't expected this. They'd been dating a year, sleeping together for less than half of that. She hadn't had a single inkling he was ready to commit his life to her.

And, of course, she'd never expected he'd be asking her to be his wife while she held a baby in her arms

"You're thinking of a dozen things right now, aren't you?" he asked. "I can practically hear your brain grinding away."

"You know me so well." She shook her head.

"Because I love you so much."

"I love you, too. More than I think I even realized until right this minute."

He tilted his head. "Is that a yes?"

She caught a corner of her lip between her teeth and, with tears starting in her eyes, asked, "Are you sure about this?" Before he could answer, she added, "Like you said, my life's a little topsy-turvy right now. Are you sure you want to take on the responsibilities of a wife, a diner, and potentially a baby, all at once? It's a lot to ask of a man. Of anyone, really."

He slid the ring from the box and wiggled his fingers for her to give him her hand. When she did, he held the ring at the tip of her fourth finger and said, "The diner comes with you, so if I want you to be my wife, I get the diner, too. In my opinion, that's a good thing. We'll always have someplace to eat, you'll have a steady income, and you can continue to honor your parents like I know you want to." He cleared his throat. "As far as a baby, this one"—he thrust his chin toward Abra—"or any other babies or children you foster, I'll treat them like our own, because they will be, Amy. And I know you want a lot of kids, your own, and ones who need you. I do, too. And I want them with you. So, to answer your question, yes. Yes I'm sure. I want you and everything that comes with you."

Those tears decided to move down Amy's cheeks while he'd been speaking.

"I want to dry your tears," he said, "but I need to do something with the ring first. So, what do you say, Amy? Will you marry me? Be mine forever? Let me love you until we're old and rickety and grumpy?"

With all the emotion clogging her throat speech was impossible, so she simply nodded and smiled.

Andy slipped the ring on her finger, then, after cupping her chin with his hands, swept her cheeks with the pads of his thumbs.

Leaning in for a kiss, he murmured against her lips, "Merry Christmas, Amy. Now, and forever."

Sighing against his lips, Amy could truly admit of all the Christmas mornings in her memory, this was the best one of all. The man she loved wanted to pledge his life to her forever, and *Santa* had brought her a baby to care for – however short or long term it would be.

Yuppers. Best Christmas morning, ever.

Dear Readers ~ I hope you enjoyed this short little glimpse in the Dickens of yesterday, circa 1983. Amy Dorrit was a favorite character of mine from ANGEL KISSES and HOLIDAY WISHES and I wanted to explore her more in depth. What I found was a woman who wanted to give back. Abra was just the first baby/child she fostered and, along with Andy, many children in Dickens found love and guidance and full bellies with these two. In future years, more of Amy's foster kids will be introduced, but first: ABRACADABRA CHARLES.

Abra's introduction in SANTA BABY sets the stage for her very own grown-up romance in FIXING CHRISTMAS, my DICKENS HOLIDAY ROMANCE coming in November 2021.

Here's a sneak peak and if you stick around, after it you can read a little from the book that introduces Amy Dorrit.

Happy reading and welcome back to Dickens.

~ Peg

FIXING CHRISTMAS – A Dickens Holiday Romance – Dorrit's Diner

"Finally," Abra Charles mumbled when the house came into view.

Exhausted from the five-hour drive on top of a six hour flight, and with a snowstorm nipping at her back bumper for the past thirty miles, Abra turned the rental car into a winding and thankfully, plowed driveway after spotting the house number on the crooked mailbox on the road.

A quick glance at the dash clock and the time of one a.m. barely registered in her tired and jet lagged brain.

Traffic had been slow and miserable the entire way from New York. Why her assistant booked her a flight to LaGuardia instead of the closer Boston airport was a matter of a serious discussion she was going to have with the girl once her brain was cleared of fatigue.

But for now she wanted something hot to drink, quick to eat, and to sleep for the next twelve hours in a comfortable bed.

And all in that order.

The house was in total darkness as she came up the drive. The one hundred year old Victorian silhouetted against the snow sky looked menacing and creepy, as if it'd stepped out of the pages of one of her books. A covered carport stood on the far side of the driveway abutting the house and Abra pulled the rental under it. Once she turned the ignition switch off she couldn't see a blessed thing in all the unnerving dark.

"Remind yourself again," she mumbled as she pulled her phone from her purse and hit the flashlight icon, "Why you thought it was a better idea to rent a house all alone out in the boonies instead of staying in town with the folks."

The reasons she needed time alone popped into her head with her next breath.

"Oh...yeah."

On a sigh filled with resignation, she alighted from the car and landed flat on her ass as her foot slipped on the icy blacktop. The thin yoga pants she'd worn to be comfortable on the long car ride and even longer flight did nothing to bar the ice from penetrating straight to her skin. The embarrassing thought of being treated at Dickens Memorial for ass frostbite had her biting back the curse that wanted desperately to shout through her lips. Reaching up, she gripped the car's door handle with her free hand, got her footing, and pulled herself into a standing position.

Her butt throbbed like a mother and stung even more.

"Welcome home, Abracadabra," she said to the silent night.

When she was certain she wouldn't take another fall, Abra let go of the door handle and reached across the front seat for her purse.

Thankfully, she hadn't dropped the phone. With it gripped in her naked hand she cursed her lack of gloves and hat, two things she didn't own and forgot to buy and bring with her in her haste to leave home. Who needed fur-lined gloves and a wool hat when they lived in Las Vegas? Sin City wasn't exactly rife with snow and frigid temps at any time of the year. Her typical daily wardrobe consisted of old T-shirts, flip flops, and the aforementioned thin yoga pants, not down jackets and snow boots.

But this was rural New England in the middle of winter. Temps below freezing, brutal wind shifts, and mountainous piles of snow were the norm here from late October to April, something she knew well since she'd grown up in the region.

After tugging her oversized suitcase and computer bag from the trunk, she slung the bag over her shoulder so she could hold her phone in one hand to light the way, and gingerly made her way to the front porch steps, a silent prayer they'd been de-iced playing on repeat in her brain. Her ass could only take so much torture.

She found the key to the rental house that was to be her home for the next month, scotch taped under the tattered welcome mat, just where her assistant stated it would be. With stiff, shaking hands growing more numb by the second, it took Abra two tries before she managed to aim the key into the lock, and another three tries before she got the partially frozen locking mechanism to turn.

The moment she stepped over the threshold the realization the inside of the house was as cold as the outside hit her like a snowball square to the face. Her breath billowed in a cloud of frost in front of her with each exhale. Stomping her feet to get some circulation back into her toes, she found the light switch on the wall and flipped it. An envelope addressed to her sat on a Chippendale table in the entranceway. Abra opened it and read the brief instructions from the realtor about the house and how to regulate the heating system, which was turned to low while the house stood vacant.

"You knew I was coming," she said to the empty room, her teeth chattering. "Why couldn't you have heated it up for me?"

But she knew the answer to that. She hadn't contacted him about her change of plans to arrive two days ahead of the scheduled agreed upon time. He hadn't known he needed to make the house warm and inviting tonight.

Probably the same reason her assistant had booked her flight to land in New York instead of Boston. Switching her arrival time, she'd had to accept whatever booking was available. Flying commercially in December was always a crapshoot, since so many people booked winter vacations, or planned to come home for the holidays from all over the country. Changing travel plans at the last minute subjected her to seat, and flight, availability.

With another sigh, this time accompanied by a jaw-widening yawn, Abra located the thermostat on the hall wall, noted the 55 degree temperature with a shiver, and reprogrammed it to seventy-five. Somewhere from the bowels of the house, the system groaned once, then rumbled to life.

It was going to take some time for the huge and rambling house to come up to a livable temperature, so Abra kept her coat on, rubbed her hands together to spark some life back into them, and went in search of the kitchen. A cup of decaf coffee would do nicely to thaw her insides while she waited for the house to warm to a life-sustaining temp.

Since the electricity was included in the cost of the rent, she had no qualms about turning on every light she passed. By the time she reached the kitchen in the back of the house, the entire downstairs was lit like the Vegas Strip at midnight.

When she'd contacted the realtor about leasing the house through the Christmas holiday and into the new year, Abra knew she'd need to set up the place to her own specifications once she arrived. That included grocery shopping. While she was welcome to eat anytime she wanted at her mom's diner, driving into Dickens three times a day didn't sound appealing. There were things she wanted stocked in the house so she could have access to them at any time of the day or night. Since she never wanted to stop working once she was on a roll, it was just easier to have available items on hand. She'd sent the realtor a detailed list and he'd promised to have them delivered before she arrived. Since she'd forgotten to email him her change in arrival plans, those items were missing when Abra searched the kitchen.

The owners of the house, the proverbial New England snowbirds, were currently spending the winter season in Florida. They'd left a pantry filled with canned goods, a stocked cleaning closet, and not much else. Sucking down a can of pork and beans at almost two in the morning wasn't in the least an appetizing thought. The refrigerator housed a of box teabags (who put those in the fridge?), a half dozen bottles of Perrier and a twelve pack of local beer. Abra preferred coffee, black, liked her water flat and never drank beer, local or otherwise.

That cup of something warm with a quick snack was going to have to wait until she could get to the grocery store in the morning.

"I wonder if the local inn has any vacancies for the night?" she asked, aloud, then shrugged. If she weren't so dog tired she'd seriously consider getting back in the car and finding out.

The house was still too cold for her liking so she kept her jacket on as she dragged her suitcase up the wide and winding stairs to the second level to find her bedroom. The realtor's note said she could use the master if she wanted to since it had an adjoining bathroom.

Even if he'd told her she couldn't, Abra had planned on procuring the master for her own since she figured the biggest and most comfortable bed would be found there. She deserved it for the price she was paying for the privilege of staying here for the month. Besides, the owners would never know she'd taken over their sleeping space. By the time they got back to town after the spring thaw she'd be long gone, the house would be spotless, and she would have eradicated any traces she'd spent time there.

The hot water took its time winding through the ancient pipes, rattling and moaning when she turned the taps on. The first trickle that dropped from the faucet was a decided golden mustard color. She turned the tap to full and within seconds the water cleared.

"If this was one of my books, none of this would bode well for the heroine," she told her image in the mirror above the sink.

While the water continued to spew and warm, Abra unpacked her essentials: toothbrush and paste, face creams, meds. After lining them up all in a row on the sink counter, she found a stocked linen closet in the hallway and pulled out several towels and washcloths. Once the water finally – *finally* – came to an acceptable warmth, she pulled back her hair and washed her face clean of the travel makeup she'd applied – *Jesus* – almost eighteen hours ago. Then, in an attempt to chase age-related wrinkles and lines away, religiously creamed her face like she did every night before bed. She hadn't shirked the nighttime ritual in twenty years no matter how tired she was.

Teeth brushed, hair as well, she debated slipping into the sleepwear she'd packed. Suddenly, too tired to even stand upright any longer, she decided to just crawl under the down comforter, fully clothed. Frank wasn't here to deride her about sleeping in her clothing, something he'd done frequently when she lost track of time while working and crashed, dressed as she was, when fatigue overcame her. No, Frank was three thousand miles west, probably having drinks at the Monte Carlo and flirting with the croupier while he gambled away the money she'd been forced to give him.

Bastard.

The sheets were cool when she slid under the covers. Thankfully, she'd had the foresight to leave her socks on. Fetaled on her side, with the comforter pulled up over her ears, Abra's last thought before sinking into a deep sleep was to wonder if the town grocery store delivered this far out.

Coming November 2021

ANGEL KISSES and HOLIDAY WISHES

A Christmas Comes To Dickens Holiday Romance

Can a first love be rekindled when the past is filled with heartache?

After a personal tragedy, Sage Hamilton left the town she'd grown up in and the boy she'd given her heart to. With a vow never to return, Sage forged on with her life in order to forget the sadness of her past.

Keith Mills loved Sage from the first moment he spotted her ambling down the hallway of their middle school. And she'd felt the same about him. Or so he'd thought until she'd walked away from everything they'd meant to one another with a tearful and rushed goodbye.

But now, eighteen years later, she's back and, as the town's new doctor, it looks like she's staying. Can Keith put the hurt of Sage's dismissal to bed for good? And will she want to rekindle the love that had burnt so bright all those years ago?

THE SOFT HUM OF INSTRUMENTAL Christmas music and the woodsy, sweet scent of newly-cut evergreen wafted around Dr. Sage Hamilton as she pushed through the front door of her favorite store in Dickens, Trim A Tree. Work obligations had forced her to leave holiday shopping until almost the last minute. Foregoing lunch, she took the hour break instead to hunt for a suitable gift for her nurse, Brianna. The young woman loved the holidays, evidenced by the addition of jingle bells to her work sneakers, the candy cane covered scrubs she'd been sporting in all colors of late, and the light-up antlers she wore whenever a pediatric patient was scheduled. Trim A Tree, Dickens' fully stocked holiday-themed store, was the perfect place to find a present special enough for the girl.

"Well now, there's my favorite doctor," Matilda Cudworth, the owner declared from her perch behind a display counter. Dressed from head to toe in a red Mrs. Claus-wannabe outfit complete with granny-style half glasses and a bonnet, Matilda's sunny smile erased the chill of the cold and cloudy December day from Sage's bones.

With a laugh, Sage shook her head while she stamped the fresh snow from her boots. "Since I'm your *personal* doctor, I'd be concerned if I *weren't* your favorite."

"True." The older woman grinned. "But I'd still like you best even if there were a thousand to choose from in this town."

The kind words went a long way in lifting Sage's spirits, which had taken a down turn once the calendar flipped to the current month. This was her first holiday season alone in over a decade and she'd been having a personal pity-party-for-one the past few days whenever her mind drifted to her present circumstances.

The decision to move back to the town she'd grown up in once her divorce was finalized had initially left Sage apprehensive. It had been almost two decades since she'd lived in Dickens and been a part of the small, tightknit community. Since she'd left town, she'd grown up, changed; matured. Would people still see her as the smart but shy teenager she'd been, or would they be able to respect her for the physician she'd become?

The town's immediate acceptance of her new role was something that helped ease her anxiety and now she had zero regrets about returning. Leaving the city she'd called home for the past ten years had been hard, but she needed a complete break in order to move on, emotionally. There were too many daily reminders in Newport of her failed marriage. She couldn't continue working in the same hospital or living in the same town as her ex. It was simply too...embarrassing.

Serendipity struck the first time she'd done an on-line physician job search once she made the decision to leave. She'd spotted the advertisement for a family doctor needed in Dickens after trolling through dozens of other job openings. A few weeks after the ink dried on her new contract, Sage packed her personal possessions and pointed her car in the direction of the town she'd left at eighteen; the place she'd vowed, once up-on a time, to never return to.

"What can I help you with today, dear?" Matilda asked.

Sage explained the special gift she wanted for her nurse.

"Nothing too cutesy," she said, "But I'd like to give her something to show her how much she means to me. Without Brianna I don't know how I'd function most days. Heck, every day. She keeps me on schedule, the patients adore her, and she truly is one of the nicest people I've ever had the good luck to work with."

Her gaze ran around the front of the chock-filled store. Jammed with holiday trees in all sizes, from three-foot table toppers to seven-foot ceiling grazers, each tree overflowed with all sizes and manner of ornaments and decorations.

A six-foot fir adorned with an assortment of teacher-themed items sat next to an evergreen filled with *firsts*: first baby, first home, first anniversary, even a first pet.

"The selection you have, Matilda, is amazing."

"Variety is the spice of life, dear. And I think I've got the perfect thing you're looking for." She moved from behind the counter to an overflowing spruce standing in front of a faux-fireplace bedecked with boughs of real holly and white lights. "Come have a look."

"Goodness." Sage's eyes widened. The tree was embellished with dozens—if not more—medical and nursing ornaments. From silver caducei, to red crosses, nursing caps to stethoscopes, every branch on the tree held something perfect for a healthcare worker. She spotted a wooden carving of a nurse holding a thermometer and a clipboard; a porcelain, bespectacled doctor standing in front of an eye chart; a woman in purple scrubs holding a swathed baby bundle in pink.

"How does anyone ever choose?" Sage asked as she ran a finger along the nurse and infant ornament.

Matilda cocked her head, the red cap shifting a tad over her bouncy white curls. "That's my specialty," she said with a smile. "I've got a knack for finding which ornament will serve best."

Matilda's startling blue eyes twinkled with moisture behind the half glasses Sage knew—for a medical fact—the older woman didn't need in order to see clearly.

"I think this one will do nicely." She gingerly removed something from the back of the tree and handed it to Sage.

In the shape of a pink scrub top, the ornament had a blank name badge over the breast pocket and a stethoscope wound around the collar. On the backside were the words, "May all the care, kindness, and love you give others come back to you a thousand fold. Thank you for all you do."

"I can inscribe Brianna's name on the badge and write a message from you under the saying, if you'd like."

Stunned, Sage replied, "It's perfect. Absolutely perfect. How did you...?" she shook her head.

The older woman's smile grew cheeky. "I've been doing this a long time, Sage. Since way before you first came into the store when you were a little girl. After a while, it's second nature to know which ornament will suit the person it's intended for."

Before she could stop herself, Sage's gaze traveled back to the nurse holding the baby.

The sadness she'd been waging a valiant fight with to keep contained threatened to seep through her resolve. With a mental shake she beat it back down.

No more gloomy thoughts. If I've learned anything this past year it's that happiness is a choice. You can either wallow in sorrow, live with regrets, or move forward.

With Christmas just two weeks away, she was determined to get through it with a smile and not mooning over the death of her marriage and lonely, childless state.

She squared her shoulders and took a cleansing breath.

When she turned back around, she found Matilda's gaze zeroed in on her. Those piercing blue eyes were pulled tight at the corners, an expression of thoughtful concern gracing her aged face. For a moment Sage wondered if the woman possessed, among her other talents, the ability to read minds.

"Is there anything else I can help you with?" she asked. "Anything else you...need?"

Someone to love me for me immediately popped into her head.

Where the heck did that come from?

She didn't dare say it out loud for fear the older woman would think her personal physician was coming unhinged. Sage could quote chapter, book, and verse on the statistics of people who mentally unraveled during the holiday season.

She cleared her throat. "This is my first Christmas...back in town," she said, grateful she'd pulled back the word *alone*, "and I need decorations for my office." With an eye roll she called up a grin. "Brianna insists I put up a tree. Said it's office tradition. Unfortunately, I didn't bring any decorations with me when I relocated and I don't have time to rummage through the attic and go through all my grandmother's old holiday boxes. Mind if I browse a bit?"

"Of course not. Take your time."

Sage wandered around the shop and picked out a dozen ornaments from various trees, each more intricate, the craftsmanship more detailed, than the next. A quick glance at her watch showed the hour she'd taken had flown by. A full compliment of afternoon patients waited for her back at the office, so with one last wistful glance at the nurse and baby ornament, she said, "I think that's it."

Matilda had engraved Brianna's gift as Sage ambled about the store. While the older woman wrapped each individual item in bubble wrap and then surrounded them with tissue paper, the shrill blare of a pager blasted from Sage's purse, competing with the piped in carols drifting from above. She bit down on her bottom lip while reading the message across the screen display.

"Problem?" Matilda asked, as she placed the purchases in a shopping bag with the store's logo.

"Emergency." She handed over her credit card. "I need to get to the hospital." After she had her receipt in hand, she added, "Thanks, again, for your help."

"I hope everything works out for you."

Sage nodded. "Your lips to God's ears."

"SHE SHOULD BE IN RECOVERY in a little over an hour," Deb Kramer, the ward nurse in charge of Corrine Mills reported. "The circulating room nurse called about five minutes ago with an update."

A banner with *Happy Holidays* hung from above the nurse's station, while gold garland wound around the workstation columns. A table-top tree bedecked with silver tinsel and a paper star sat front and center on the ward clerk's desk.

"I'm going to order a battery of tests for her once she's stabilized from the surgery. Her blood pressure came down some in the ER from the initial 200 over 110 reading the paramedics took. Since Corrine has a history of hypertension that's been controlled well," Sage said, "I need to figure out what caused the spike."

"Has her grandson been notified?" Deb asked. Sage's eyes were drawn to the pin of Rudolf and his blinking red nose Deb had affixed to her scrub top.

"Corrine's maid, Maria, called him. He said he was getting the first plane he could."

"My guess, for what it's worth?" Deb signed off on the chart in her hand and placed it back in the rolling rack of patient charts. "He'll charter a private one to get here as fast as he can. It's not like he can't afford it, and Mrs. Mills means everything to him."

Even though she hadn't seen, nor spoken, to Keith Mills in almost twenty years, Sage knew what a successful man he'd become. The first time Corrine walked into her office for a routine checkup, the older woman brought her up to speed on her only grandchild's accomplishments, regaling Sage with stories about his architectural firm and the myriad of important projects he'd been involved with around the world.

"Make sure someone pages me when he gets here," Sage instructed. "I'm going down to medical records to do some charting."

"Will do."

Brianna had rearranged Sage's afternoon schedule in order to deal with Corrine Mills' emergency. One of the best parts of coming back home had been reconnecting with Corinne. Since the passing of her own grandmother and mother, Sage had missed the wisdom and counseling of the women who'd helped mold her into the person she was today. Corrine Mills, with her ready shoulder to lean on and ears meant for listening, had been the perfect person for Sage to reconnect with.

Of course, hearing all Corrine's accolades about the man Sage had once loved was a bit...unsettling. But she'd put on a happy face and let the old woman brag to her heart's content.

Keith Mills.

He'd filled so many *firsts* in Sage's life, reminding her of the ornament tree in Matilda's shop. First kiss, first boyfriend, first love...and lover.

He'd also been the first man her heart had broken over.

Oh, well. All that's in the past. He probably hasn't even thought about me since I left town.

When she signed off on her last chart, the beeper attached to her lab coat vibrated.

~Keith Mills is here.

Dragging in a calming breath, Sage mentally prepared herself to see the man she'd left standing in angry and emotional tatters eighteen years ago.

She heard him before she ever laid eyes on him.

"Where's my grandmother's doctor?" he bellowed from the nurse's station. "Get him up here right now."

"I already paged Dr. Hamilton," Deb said, her voice staying calm and controlled.

Sage stopped as she turned the hallway corner and spotted Keith.

He was impossible to miss.

From his impressive and imposing six-foot-three height he towered above the diminutive nurse as he stood, arms akimbo, glaring down his nose at her.

An annoyed scowl twisted his mouth, but the memory of how seductive and alluring those full lips could be when pulled into a wicked grin burned bright in her mind.

"Where's Doc Martin? He's been my grandmother's physician for decades. Who is this Hamilton person?"

"Keith."

No amount of preparation could have prevented the full effect of Keith Mills' gaze from shooting through Sage when he turned to her.

As a teenager he'd been all gangly arms and monkey hands, bony shoulders and narrow hips. His face had yet to fill out, but even back then his features hinted at a classic, movie star handsomeness to come.

As a man now, he'd outgrown the teen gauntness and his body had settled into perfect male proportions. Those bony shoulders spanned a yard and dropped into arms bulging underneath a fitted shirt. That hint of good looks had blossomed into a face sculpted by the gods of gorgeous. Cheekbones cut from glass sat over a square and powerful jaw. All in all, he'd grown into one magnificent man.

Damn him.

Whatever he'd been about to say died before he gave it a voice. In the span of a heartbeat his expression went from annoyed to confused, his eyes widening, then the corners pulling into a squint, his lips lifting from their frown to form a wide O of surprise.

"Sage?" Incredulity graced his voice – a man's voice. Rich and deep; hard and commanding. A shiver of intense and unexpected longing zipped down her spine at the timbre.

She swallowed and beat back the panicked nerves tumbling through her system. "It's been a long time." She walked toward the nurse's station, her gaze steadier than her trembling hands.

Indecision blasted through her the nearer she came. Be professional and shake his hand, or hug him like a long lost friend?

"What are you doing here?"

The irritation behind his question decided her response. She clasped her quivering hands in front of her and said, "You wanted to speak to me about your grandmother. Why don't we go down to the cafeteria to talk? Corrine's still in surgery and it's going to be a bit before you can see her."

Slipping her hands into her lab coat pockets, she tilted her head, indicating for him to follow as she began walking toward the elevator bank.

"*Wait.*"

She stopped, mid stride, and turned back around.

"I don't understand." He shook his head, his eyebrows lifting to his hairline. "*You're* my grandmother's physician? *You're...*Dr. Hamilton?"

Don't miss out!

Visit the website below and you can sign up to receive emails whenever Peggy Jaeger publishes a new book. There's no charge and no obligation.

https://books2read.com/r/B-A-NSGN-EINOB

BOOKS 2 READ

Connecting independent readers to independent writers.

About the Author

Peggy Jaeger is a contemporary romance writer who writes Romantic Comedies about strong women, the families who support them, and the men who can't live without them. If she can make you cry on one page and bring you out of tears rolling with laughter the next, she's done her job as a writer! Family and food play huge roles in Peggy's stories because she believes there is nothing that holds a family structure together like sharing a meal...or two...or ten. Dotted with humor and characters that are as real as they are loving, she brings all topics of daily life into her stories: life, death, sibling rivalry, illness and the desire for everyone to find their own happily ever after. Growing up the only child of divorced parents she longed for sisters, brothers and a family that vowed to stick together no matter what came their way. Through her books, she's created the families she wanted as that lonely child. When she's not writing Peggy is usually painting, crafting, scrapbooking or decoupaging old steamer trunks she finds at rummage stores and garage sales. As a lifelong diarist, she caught the blogging bug early on, and you can visit her at peggyjaeger.com where she blogs daily about life, writing, and stuff that makes her go "What??!"

Read more at https://peggyjaeger.com/.

Made in the USA
Columbia, SC
12 November 2024

45936794R00038